The Tanzania Juma

Juma's Dhow Race

by Lisa Maria Burgess

illustrated by Abdul M. Gugu

Hello. My name is Juma. I am Tanzanian. My *Baba* is from the island of Zanzibar and my *Mama* is from the mainland of Tanzania. Like a little rabbit, I am super quick and full of tricks, so my parents call me *Super Sungura*. But most of the time, I am just Juma—Ijumaa when *Mama* wants to be serious.

Guess what? I like swimming.

Guess what, what? My sister Sareeya and I are going to visit our family in Zanzibar and *Babu* promises to give us more swimming lessons. Cousin Akida (that one who doesn't like to share), his brother, Mrefu, and their new baby are going too. Our *babas*' brother, the one they call *Ndugu Samaki*, will race in the Zanzibar Dhow Race.

So today we are packing our bags and getting ready for the ferry. *Mama* is running around, shouting *haraka, haraka*, quick, quick!

In the morning we get up early.

Baba carries the bags and *Mama* holds our hands while we stand in line for the tickets. Then we find seats and wait for everyone to get on.

I have to sit with Akida. He hits me in the stomach with his elbow. He pretends it was an accident. *Baba* says, "Stop complaining Ijumaa, and show your elder brother respect." I know that Akida is only older than me by a few weeks, but I listen to *Baba* and keep my mouth shut.

This is going to be a looooong ferry ride.

We spend the night at *Babu*'s home. My favorite room is the kitchen because it has two million spices. I like smelling the cloves and the cinnamon and the cardamom.

Guess what? I have to share a bed with Akida.

Guess what, what? He doesn't share that cover with me. But, really, it's too hot for covers!

We get up early again the next morning. We follow our *babas* to the harbor. The streets are so skinny that only people can walk in them. Even bicycles have trouble squeezing through.

I say, "My *Baba* is the one who knows the way." Akida says, "My *Baba* is the one who really knows the way." Mama tells us we are worse than the crows. She takes us each by the hand.

We follow our *babas*, who are walking with *Babu* quick, quick through the puzzle streets.

*N*dugu Samaki takes us in his dhow to Changuu Island. We are going to see the tortoises and watch the race.

Mama makes me sit next to her, away from Akida. I want to tell her that it is Akida who gives trouble, but I remember what *Baba* said and I keep very quiet. I am so quiet that *Mama* forgets to hold my hand.

At Changuu Island, Sareeya jumps off the dhow. She wants to see the tortoises.

She shouts, "Where are you Mr. and Mrs. *Kobe*?" and runs up the beach.

The babas and mamas and cousins all run after her across the sandy beach.

I hide behind a box in the dhow. I don't want any more trouble with that cousin of mine. I don't even care if I see the tortoises. I just want to be alone.

I curl up and hide— nice and quiet. I think about how sorry *Mama* will be when she finds that I am gone. I think about how my *Shangazi* will yell at Akida for not being nice to me.

Ndugu Samaki doesn't see me. He sails the dhow away from Changuu Island and back to Stone Town.

The waves move the dhow up and down. Soon I am asleep.

I wake up when *Ndugu Samaki* starts shouting orders. The wind is making noises in the sail.

I stand up and see that we are back at Stone Town. There are two times twenty dhows, and there are at least four times twenty sailors rushing their dhows from the sand beach into the sea.

Suddenly the race has started!

The wind catches the sail. The dhow jerks forward and I fall overboard. Splash!

I don't know if I remember how to swim.

I try to remember what *Babu* always tells me. I put my nose in the air and move my hands quickly like a puppy. I tell myself that I am just like a little Mr. *Mbwa* out for a swim.

Lucky for me, *Ndugu Samaki* sees me and turns his dhow around. He pulls me out by my shirt and sets me on the floor. He rushes to get back in the race.

When I stop coughing, I look around.

Ndugu Samaki is not happy to see me. He is not happy at all that I fell in the water and slowed down his dhow. The wind is pushing on the sail. He and the sailor are working hard to catch the other dhows.

I remember to be polite. I ask *Ndugu Samaki* how I can help. At first he doesn't listen, then he looks me up and down. He says, "If you really want to help, get out on that pole and help balance the wind."

I am just a tiny, tiny bit scared, but I can't say no. I crawl on the wooden pole that sticks out straight over the waves. I balance. I tell myself, slowly, slowly, *pole, pole*!

Sareeya is having fun. She is racing after giant hundred year old Mr. and Mrs. *Kobe*.

Mama says they came long ago in a dhow from the Seychelles—that's another country in case you don't know.

Sareeya and Akida and Mrefu feed the tortoises their lettuce. Then they race to count the babies in their little house.

Baba and *Mama* are chasing that *Little Sungura*. When *Baba* finally catches her, he slips in some of that green tortoise poop. He slips and slips, and slides!

Baba cleans up in the bathroom and they walk out on the boardwalk. Sareeya tells me later that this is when they wonder where I am.

Baba asks where is that *Super Sungura*. *Mama* says last she remembers Ijumaa was sitting quietly in the dhow. *Shangazi* says maybe I am with the tortoises.

Sareeya spots me first. She jumps up and down and points. She shouts, "*Hujambo Ndugu Samaki! Hujambo Kaka Juma!*"

Look at everyone jump and wave when they see me sail!

I am a tiny, tiny bit less scared, so I wave back.

We sail around Changuu Island and back to Stone Town, where *Babu* is waiting for us.

Guess what? The wind blowing and the water splashing is fun.

Guess what, what? *Ndugu Samaki* comes in second place. He puts me on his shoulders and dances in the sand.

Babu says I am another fish just like my uncle. He says I am the next generation of *samaki*.

I don't tell him that I still swim like a puppy. Next time *Babu* gives me a swimming lesson, I will listen very, very carefully!

Tanzania

Juma lives in Dar es Salaam in the east African country of Tanzania.

Tanzania stretches east to the beaches of the Zanzibar islands, west to the plains of the mainland, south to Lake Tanganyika, and north to Lake Victoria and the peak of Mount Kilimanjaro.

People in his family speak ki-Swahili and English, as well as ki-Sukuma and other languages. Juma likes to repeat words, which is a habit in ki-Swahili: In English we might say something like “very slow”, but in ki-Swahili we would say *pole, pole* (“slow, slow”).

Tanzania is famous for all sorts of wonderful things – the spices grown in Zanzibar, the coffee and tea grown in the highlands and the cotton in the lowlands, the purple, blue stone called Tanzanite found deep in the earth, and of course the wild animals that live in the national parks.

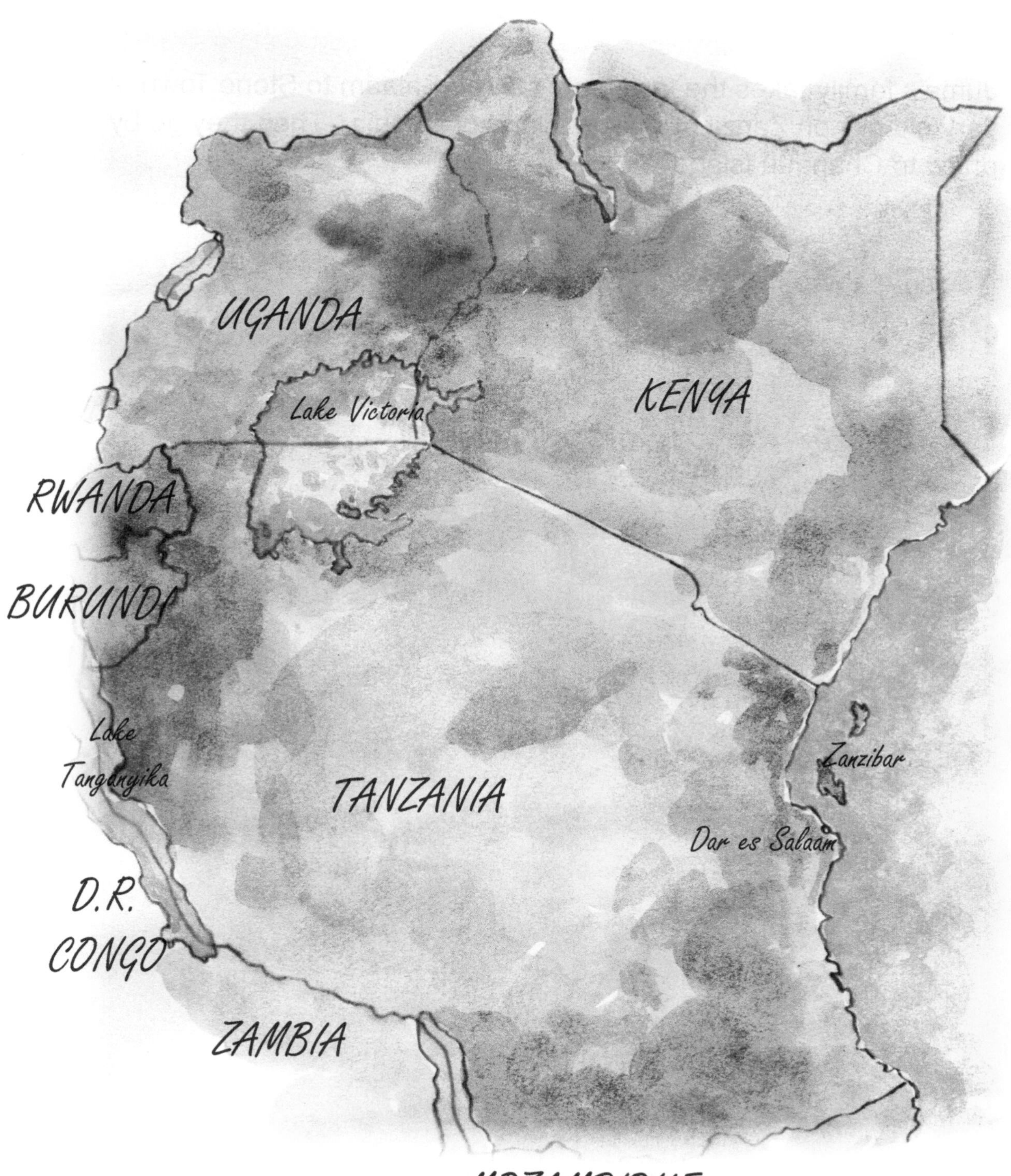
UGANDA
KENYA
Lake Victoria
RWANDA
BURUNDI
Lake
Tanganyika
TANZANIA
Zanzibar
Dar es Salaam
D.R.
CONGO
ZAMBIA
MOZAMBIQUE

Zanzibar

Juma's family takes the ferry from Dar es Salaam to Stone Town, a very old city on Zanzibar's main island of Unguja. Then they go by dhow to Changuu Island.

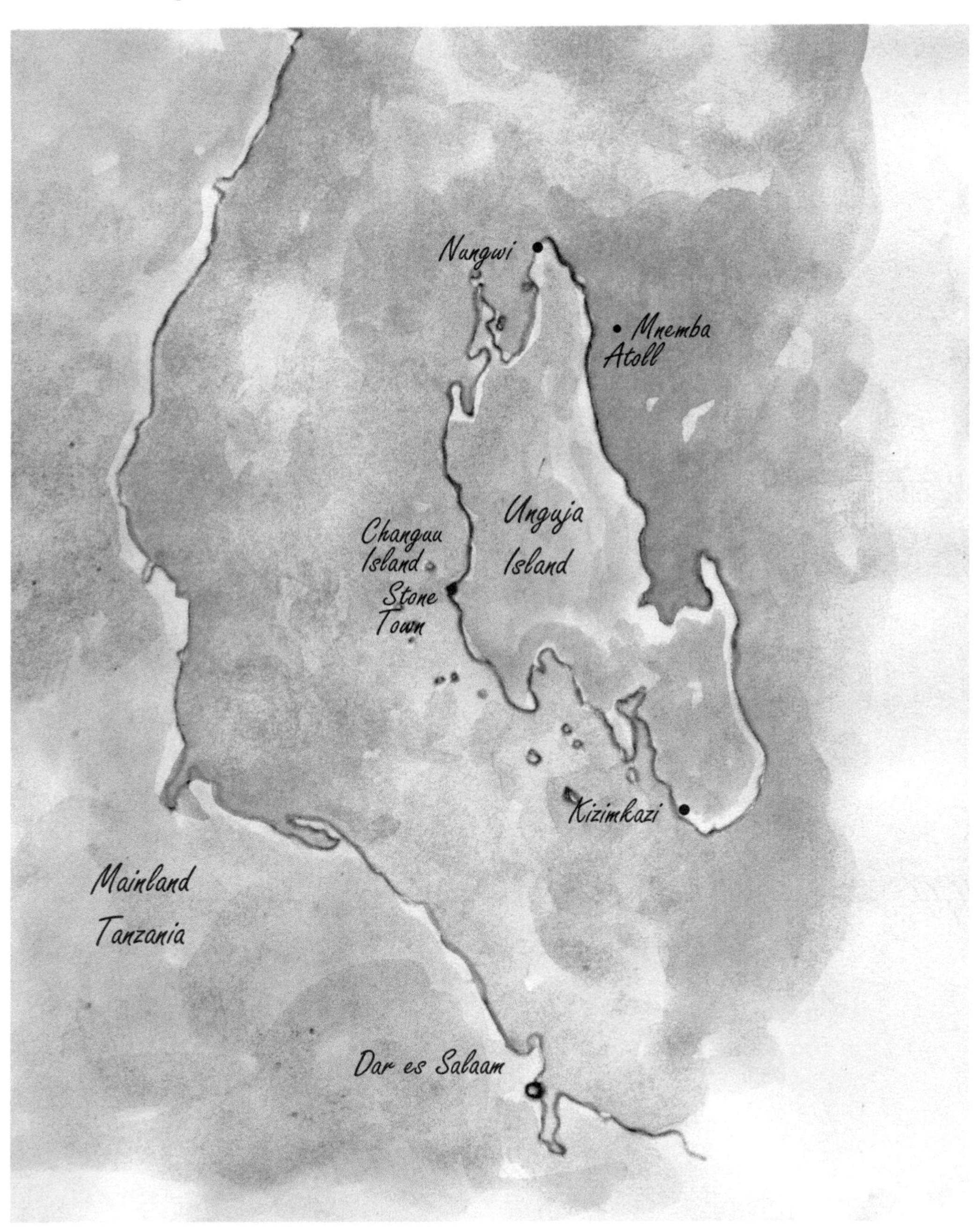

The Dhow

The dhow is a boat with one or more lateen sails.

There are different sized dhows. Some are small and used for fishing. Others are big and used to transport goods and people up and down the east coast of Africa. One that is ten meters long, for example, can carry twenty-five passengers. The smaller five-meter dugout uses outriggers to provide balance.

Dhows are often built in Nungwi, on the north side of Zanzibar.

Some sailors sail their dhows from island to island in the Zanzibar archipelago, but others go as far north as the Persian Gulf.

Ki-Swahili and English Glossary:

Baba:	Father or Paternal Uncle
Babu:	Grandfather
Dhow:	East African boat with a lateen sail used for fishing and transport
Haraka:	Quick
Hujambo:	Greeting (hello)
Kaka:	Brother (older)
Kobe:	Tortoise
Mama:	Mother
Mbwa:	Dog
Ndugu Samaki:	Brother Fish
Pole, pole:	Slowly, slowly (carefully)
Shangazi:	Paternal Aunt
Sungura:	Rabbit

About the Authors:

At the time of writing these stories, **Lisa Maria Burgess** taught in the Department of Literature at the University of Dar es Salaam. She wrote the Juma stories with her sons, **Matoko** and **Senafa**.

About the Illustrator:

Abdul M. Gugu lives in Dar es Salaam where he works as an illustrator of children's books and as an artist.

 For information, address Barranca Press, Taos, New Mexico, USA via editor@barrancapress.com.
Designed by LMB Noudehou. Cover design by Sarah Markes.
www.barrancapress.com

FIRST EDITION, July 2013

ISBN 978-1-939604-05-7

Library of Congress Catalog Card Number: 2013937629

Manufactured in the United States of America.

CPSIA information can be obtained at www.ICGtesting.com
Printed in the USA
LVOW020738050713

341496LV00001B/4/P